The illustrations for this book were done in acrylic, ink, and pencil on plywood.
This book was edited by Megan Tingley and Bethany Strout
and designed by Saho Fujii with art direction by Patti Ann Harris.
The production was supervised by Erika Schwartz, and the production editor was Christine Ma.
The text was set in Gararond Medium and the display type is Aram Caps.
This book was printed on uncoated paper.

Copyright © 2014 by Naoko Stoop • Cover art © 2014 by Naoko Stoop • Cover design by Saho Fujii • Cover © 2014 Hachette Book Group, Inc. • All rights reserved. In accordance with the U.S. Copyright Act of 1976, the scanning, uploading, and electronic sharing of any part of this book without the permission of the publisher is unlawful piracy and theft of the author's intellectual property. If you would like to use material from the book (other than for review purposes), prior written permission must be obtained by contacting the publisher at permissions@hbgusa.com. Thank you for your support of the author's rights. • Little, Brown and Company • Hachette Book Group • 237 Park Avenue • New York, NY 10017 • Visit our website at lb-kids.com • Little, Brown and Company is a division of Hachette Book Group, Inc. • The Little, Brown name and logo are trademarks of Hachette Book Group, Inc. • The publisher is not responsible for websites (or their content) that are not owned by the publisher. • First Edition: September 2014 • Library of Congress Cataloging-in-Publication Data • Stoop, Naoko, author, illustrator. • Red Knit Cap Girl and the reading tree / by Naoko Stoop.—First edition. • pages cm • Summary: Red Knit Cap Girl and her animal friends create a library inside a mighty oak tree, where they can read and exchange books. • ISBN 978-0-316-22886-2 (hardcover) • 1. Books and reading—Juvenile fiction. 2. Libraries—Juvenile fiction. 3. Forest animals—Juvenile fiction. 4. Sharing—Juvenile fiction. [1. Books and reading—Fiction. 2. Libraries—Fiction. 3. Forest animals—Fiction. 4. Sharing—Fiction.] 1. Title. • PZ7.S88353Rf 2014 • [E]—dc23 • 2013034964 • 10 9 8 7 6 5 4 3 2 1 • SC • Printed in China

RED KNIT CAP GIRL AND THE READING TREE

by NAOKO STOOP

Megan Tingley Books
LITTLE, BROWN AND COMPANY
New York   Boston

It is too hot to run and too hot to play. Red Knit Cap Girl and White Bunny find a shady spot and read.

Squirrel wants to show them something, but he won't tell them what.
"You'll see when we get there" is all he will say.

Red Knit Cap Girl and White Bunny scamper after Squirrel.

"What a big oak tree," Red Knit Cap Girl says when Squirrel points.
"Not the tree," Squirrel says. "Look inside."

Red Knit Cap Girl looks inside the hole in the trunk.
"That's what I wanted to show you all,"
Squirrel says. "It's called a nook."

"What is it for?" says Bear.

Red Knit Cap Girl listens to the leaves rustling
and feels the soft grass under her feet.
She looks again at the nook.
"I have an idea," she says.

Red Knit Cap Girl puts her book inside,
where it will stay safe and dry.
"I will keep my book in this nook so everyone can
read it," Red Knit Cap Girl says.
"I will keep my book in this nook so everyone can
read mine, too," White Bunny says.

"I will, too!" says Squirrel.
"Great idea!" Bear cheers.

Hedgehog is too excited to speak.
He just squeaks. *"Eek, eek!"*

The Birds swoop down.
"We have something to share, too!"

"I don't have a book," Beaver says sadly. He wants to share something.

Then Beaver gets an idea.

He gnaws and hauls with his teeth and thumps with his tail until he's built a strong bookshelf.

Everyone admires it.

The next day, Deer brings his book to the nook.
Duck follows with her book.

Turtle has so many books to share
that she carries them on her back!

Sly Fox doesn't help. She sneaks to the nook when she thinks no one is looking. "How silly they are, leaving all these books here for me to steal," she says as she takes one.

The other animals bring more books to the nook. They read every
day until the air turns clear and crisp and cold. It is autumn now,
too cold to sit still around the nook.

"Snuggle under these!" the Sheep say.
They've made warm wool blankets for everyone.
Then the nook is even cozier.

All summer, all fall, Owl and Moon have been watching
Red Knit Cap Girl and her friends. Now it is almost winter.
Days are shorter, and dark comes earlier. Owl and Moon
talk in hushed voices about what Red Knit Cap Girl
and her friends have done.
"We can help, too!" Moon says, and she tells Owl how.

They work all night long.

In the morning, Red Knit Cap Girl and her friends see
what Owl has made for them.
Red Knit Cap Girl reads the sign out loud.
"'Library,'" she says. "A library is a place where
anyone can borrow a book."
Red Knit Cap Girl winks at Sly Fox,
who smiles shyly back.

That night, Moon shines her light on the nook and the friends read. Sly Fox returns the book she took, and Red Knit Cap Girl reads it out loud to everyone.

"Thank you, Red Knit Cap Girl," say the little ones who can't read yet. "Thank *you*, Deer, Bear, Birds, Duck, Squirrel, Hedgehog, Beaver, Sheep, Turtle and turtle babies, Sly Fox, Owl, White Bunny, and Moon. Thank you for making our library," says Red Knit Cap Girl.

"It is good to share books."